BANDED ROCKS

AND OTHER POEMS

SOUMYA ADHIKARI

Copyright © Soumya Adhikari
All Rights Reserved.

This book has been published with all efforts taken to make the material error-free after the consent of the author. However, the author and the publisher do not assume and hereby disclaim any liability to any party for any loss, damage, or disruption caused by errors or omissions, whether such errors or omissions result from negligence, accident, or any other cause.

While every effort has been made to avoid any mistake or omission, this publication is being sold on the condition and understanding that neither the author nor the publishers or printers would be liable in any manner to any person by reason of any mistake or omission in this publication or for any action taken or omitted to be taken or advice rendered or accepted on the basis of this work. For any defect in printing or binding the publishers will be liable only to replace the defective copy by another copy of this work then available.

8

To all those

to who a warm tight hug

would suffice to give

a wholeness in the

meaning of

their life.

8

Contents

Acknowledgements

This book is concisely the result of the both direct and indirect contributions of the people in my life. First among those who have inspired, encouraged, and helped me are my friends, Anusmita Sarkar, Ishan Dey, etc. A special thanks to Swatilakha Saha, who has helped me in several phases of the process of publication.

My deep gratitude is to all my teachers, especially Laki Molla, Ms. Janki Singh, Hindol Palit, Sri Mandip Chakraborty, etc., for their guidance in analysing and observing, which took me to a juncture of ideas. I also thank them for their feedback and for being in my constant support.

My mother, Mithu Adhikary, whose life is a treasure of tales, is my source of motivation. I am grateful and thankful to her for caring for me with her loving nature, gentle and benign behavior, and for always believing in me.

I would also like to thank Notionpress for providing me with the opportunity to publish this book.

Soumya Adhikari

PREFACE

I would like to employ the opportunity to write the things and notions expressively which drove me to write these prose and poems and also, I shall put my arguments in the response to what I have already got. If we consider first, the prose which is named "Banded Rocks" is purely a geographical term which is related to the process of metamorphism. Sometimes minerals and materials of different groups are arranged into alternating thin to thick layers, appearing in light and dark shades. Such a structure in metamorphic rocks is called 'banding' and rocks displaying banding are called 'banded rocks.' It is what I have tried to apply metaphorically. Basically, if the structure of the prose is analysed acutely, perhaps what I am trying to convey may be understood. Certainly, it should not be perceived of what I say is the last say or *ultima verba*. There may be or are possibly other ways to see it.

It is an independent text, though there is a portion that directly deals with Henrik Ibsen's *A Doll's House.* I would refer to it time and again during the course of writing. It should not be assumed that in any way I have tried to disrespect the feminists' movement to emancipate themselves from being crushed under the malevolent patriarchy. Nora's journey is exceptional as it has been from being an idealist to a 'lone realist' as envisaged by George Bernard Shaw in *Quintessence of Ibsenism.* Nora only exception in the whole play. Moreover, it can also be said that she is the only exception in that contemporary society too. To some people, an exception is not an example. However, an exception sets an example, showing that there are other ways around it. By which I mean to say that an exception is, very much in degree, an example, which beckons that there is/are alternate possibility/ies. Therefore, it implies that an exception is the first example.

However, my self-written prose differs from the play written by Ibsen, in several aspects, and neither the mother, that women character takes the central stage, though almost every plot hovers around her. Most important, the mother, who I depict in my story, is not an exception. There are millions of examples who can be found who are in conditions like her, and I have only added one to those millions. What is exceptional, if it needs to be said, is only that the story is set in a different and contemporary socio-cultural and political milieu. Chinua Achebe once said, "It is the storyteller, who makes us what we are, who creates history. The storyteller creates the memory that the survivor must have— otherwise their surviving would have no meaning. " I have tried to display the *raison d'être* of their existence.

I was overwhelmed by the depiction of Bertha Maison/ Antoinette in Jean Rhys' *Wide Sargasso Sea*; the transition from Bertha to Antoinette; the tragedies that led her to be a lunatic and to become an 'other' in *Jane Eyre*. Another short story, if I may consider, is of Bessie Head's *The Collector of Treasures*, a tragedy met by Dikeledi Mokopi. Both the novels are very realistic in their depiction. Cruel realities were brought to the surface, that they were not born like that, but they were moulded by various circumstances which made them to become like that and act like that. Although this prose does not reach these extremes, this is, in a way, also a tragedy, but not a conventional one. Like all these postcolonial literary pieces, adding to the different shades of reality, this story also adds to the reality of another postcolonial world. This unnamed woman has almost everything; a share in the public domain, land, property, education (though not through an easy ongoing process), and even, to an extent, the law stands by her, which can be analysed, when she implies in a serious argument with her husband indirectly. Then why is she living such a painful life which gives her almost nothing? The answer, I think, is embedded in another character who is preferably the protagonist of this story.

The mother in this story has the financial control that Nora did not have. Things are way more complicated than they look, and than that Ibsen manifests in his play. Leaving in an instant was an option for Nora. However, it does not seem that to leave is an option for this woman. She confirms the fact, I think, that she does not want her son to become Torvald or Garesgo or a carbon copy of his own father.

If we look at the father, no doubt he is abusive and irresponsible, but we need to think and reconsider the father as he is also a victim of this society. He is also an economically 'other' character. He has not got the education which he should have. He is also betrayed and deprived by his own close relations. These are not, in any way, excuses or justifications for his abusive, rude behaviour and carelessness. However, the mother understands these and is compassionate and sympathetic towards her child, just as the child is towards her. She knows that he has no one except her. The cycle of deprivation, lovelessness, and of becoming the same nefarious product may not be broken. This is what reality is. When she has really taken the onus onto her shoulder, we can do nothing except appreciating her. Although the story is claimed to be fictional, the elements are drawn from our own society.

Now, think of the boy, preferably the protagonist of the story, who turns to literature to express his heart out. The writing of his own story is completely getting amalgamated with the narration of his surroundings. It is a story, if it is technically called, a coming-of-age or a bildungsroman. There are brief moments where a third-person narrator advents and speaks on behalf of the boy. The basic intention was to imply that it is the voice of the same boy who is suffering from the dilemma of letting know the things he is hesitant about. He turns to literature to talk about his mother, if we suppose, and lets us know his own insights about literature while describing the things about his mother. However, he is insecure not only because of his family tragedy, but he can also be perceived as a person who is sexually 'other'. He is quite rebellious against the hetero-normative social structure. He subtly and ambiguously inserts his own self into his speeches, particularly when arguing that he will not have any "dasyus," which his mother understands and misinterprets as a beckoning that his children will not be mischievous. However, his mother misses the point that what he may be trying to espouse is that he can not have any biological children. Therefore, all three are struck in one way or the other.

———————

Sexual 'otherness' is not applicable to the prose portion only. There are even poems that directly deal with this.

All poems are written in blank verse and many among them have allusions from Greek and Indian mythologies.

There is one particular poem written in memory of my late friend who passed away so tragically, and we were very close friends.

There are other poems too, written following the principles of 'the disassociation of personality' of T. S. Eliot.

There are poems which are monologue, and expedition of mind through 'stream of consciousness'. However, there are poems that are written out of personal emotions too. What is common in both prose and poems is the use of Indian English, especially of Bengali terms and connotations, which implies and vivifies the setting and gives a Bengali aura.

Literature, to what I believe, takes its proper shape in one's hand when the person is emotionally affluent and has experiences, which definitely comes from acute and meticulous observations and to which age is merely a factor. The method or the way of observation is learned as well, and most often it seems that we are induced by our surrounding factors. By which I also mean, that even when we observe, we choose to observe our preferred things, and what we choose to observe is, in most cases, what is already in some way familiar to us. We develop our ideas, notions, and ideologies from our socio-cultural milieu. To a very large extent, our mentality, and psyche are also the victims of our environment. As Emile Zola correctly pointed out that we are the products of our environment. After we have an understanding of our lives, of how we get induced and obstructed, and to what extent we are, we fight back. It is the fight we choose to fight by juxtaposing various contradictory ideas which go against the previously acquired ideas. It is a continuous process with hardly any interval and is hardly in our control sometimes. It requires labour and strong determination to free ourselves from the shackle of ourselves previously formed.

Howsoever, when we try, we evolve, though sometimes we evolve not so deliberately as everything depends on the individual charisma or everything is decided by external factors profoundly, can not be said. This book implies that

I have tried, even if the writing may be considered at its nascent stage. I may change my stance in the rare future, but now I am really happy that I can reach you through this debut book of mine.

I wish every reader a happy reading.
Soumya Adhikari.
Kolkata, 2022.

PART A

BANDED ROCKS

I

'Everybody has stories to tell. So do I.'

" *Maa, baba* is coming, I can hear it."

"Open the door."

"Wait...I am busy now."

" Arr...dhurr... eat the mangoes later, Open the DOOR FIRST."

Instead of letting the tussle to go on, and to save every bricks of the house from being shaken terribly, I woke and opened the door for him.

I sat and tried to write again.

"Everybody has stories to tell. So do I. Everybody has a lot of stories but it is about his or her personal choice whether he would share it or not. The matter does not only stick to sharing, it's about how to share, and where to share."

The whole house scents of something conflicting, tumultuous, the foulness of this smell goes parallel to that of my father's hard laborious stinky sweat. It intensifies when my father comes home. I can hear the ominous throat has opened but running in a stable voice,---

" I have to be home tomorrow, none can give me work, if it goes on like this, I would be in home in upcoming week as well."

"Hasn't even Nitin da stored anything?"

"No, no one, I think I have to look for something else. I can not go on like this."

"Ok. Eat the rest after you wash yourself; it's for you two."

I went up there and finished my part. *Baba* cleaned the area aftermath with water and heard---

"Prepare the salad, I'm almost ready to serve dinner."

After I had dinner, I heard *baba* whispering something to *maa*...

"Amit says I have to pay nothing except registration fee. Only some documents will do."

"Where will you drive then?"

"In the streets of Kolkata, I'll have map."

"How much he earns?"

"He earns more than 500 rupees even though he drives only till afternoon."

II

ONE DAY LATER

"So, tell me where are you facing problem?"

"Sir, could you please tell me whether a text can be misinterpreted or not?"

"No, there is nothing called misinterpretation in literature. It's the beauty of literature, you know, you can have your own perspective as well. The meaning of a text is multi-layered. Do you know what Roland Barthes says in his essay "The Death of the Author"?"

" The birth of the reader must be ransomed by the death of the author."

"' The unity of a text is not in it's origin, it is in it's destination." Before it he says " he is in no way the subject of which his book is the predicate.'"

"Yeah, I have read it."

"You know this well then, in addition to this we do not consider anything wrong in art, we consider the mistake as beautiful. Literature differs from mathematics; we do not count two plus two is four, rather we take the possibility of having five adding two to two. It may produce three as well. What we do is give space to both or multiple coexisting thoughts or narratives. Didn't I tell you these before? One thing we may do is to contextualise the art, the continuum in which the art was produced. We may not do it ofcourse. Tell me truly, have you ever been convinced by my explanation completely. I can bet, No! You are never convinced...

(Laughter)

You are never convinced completely. I see you, while I teach you. If you do not agree to my point you just remain head down but if you do you shake your head with a shock."

(Laughter) "I thought you do not contact anyone's eyes when you teach."

"Yeah, you know, I have become accustomed to it through the years. I can see everything even when you think I am not looking at you.

It's already the end of the session, it wouldn't be of much difficulty to tell me that---

Do you find inconsistency when I speak?"

"What I think is that sir, you have inconsistency and that is something normal. We all have inconsistency. Sometimes we go too far to contradict ourselves. It's because our lives are not linear. The path we go on is not linear. Even the usage of the word 'path' is suitable or not is very much a doubt. We in no way can describe our things in a single theory."

"True. True ..."

"I doubt sir, whether literature can be taken that much lighter... I mean the author writes something to let something know or to express to the mass but what if I presume what author has written is very surface level interpretation, what if I do not like how the author has presented a thing."

"If you go to a library, and if you do not find the book you are searching for, write your own book. It is what Toni

Morrison has said, I am actually echoing that. Do it, go, write your own book."

III

"Arr...Do I know you? Ain't you and I of same school?"

"Yes, you were one year junior to me. You're Dhruva, right?"

"Yes, what are you doing here?"

"I went to tuition, waiting for train."

"So, how everything is going, all good?"

"Yeah, yours?"

"Yeah, all good. How many girlfriends do you have now, *han* ?

"I do not have any, may be I'll not have any."

"Why?" (touching the biceps) "So sexy biceps you have got"

"Do not talk nonsense, we are in public"

"yeah, I am speaking nonsense hann!

"You are still immature."

"Ooh... Now I am immature hann."

It feels like shit, when these assholes turn up. Ruined my whole school life. Every single day I had to hear in every aspects of my life that how I am different from them. I can make this understand to you people because you are reading but what about them! They feel it something funny, if they got you like this they would ridicule, they would bully, and literature to them is something of alien land, even if they read, they will use for tagging that they have read it. But they would hardly try to understand anything. Again turned up to ruin my day.

"Do you know any of your friends what they are doing?"

"I know some. Some of them had got into D. U., J.N.U., R.I.E., some are in IITs, NITs, and some are doing graduation from their local college like me. I do not want to keep contact with any of those of my school."

"So, would you like to take this train? I'm going, I'm not seeking your phone number then as you said..."

"Yeah..."

"Do you not live in my way?"

"Yeah, I live, but I'll not take this train, you go."

Just FUCK OFF......

"Ok, Bye."

"Yeah, bye."

Few minutes later, I took the train. Every time when I am in train, and I look at other people, I feel very angry and get irritated for my mother. My mother does not believe me that I use my headphone when I am at safe place. I'm not like other millennials. But it's good to see the beauty outside and how much the usual has changed with new incorporations. I do not find much. It's all the same.

As usual, my mother is not at home. Because you know, my mother has to go office. I enjoy this little time. I do not hurry much when I am in road. But I do when I see a big lock has been hanging on the front door. I rushed in to lock the door from inside. You know, I enjoy this little time. You can watch porn or a movie or you can get naked, or sing a song, or dance while listening anything, anything you want. You do not have to hide anything because you are watching something impermissible or you do not have to feel embarrass for anything you are acting. All the theories, ideologies, notions, thoughts, evaporates this time from my head. Outer world has no significance. I am completely left with my own. But what I did in this little time on that day you should not know too. Only thing I can tell you is that I felt very tired and I slept until my mother woke me up.

Believe me, I had clear intention of writing that I wanted to but I missed something. Not having any two at home, my own smell spread so much that I couldn't get the smell of something ominous.

Since my childhood this is the first time my mother told me that she wants divorce. I got completely shaken. I felt like I am just an empty shell and has been squeezed thoroughly to produce juice. Lately my father can not raise his voice to imply something to my mother when I'm around. My father has found this time in the morning to quarrel when my mother is totally left alone. I know who the guilty is, and who does not care much, I know. But you know I cannot tell him everything, not because I do not have the capability to say the thing which I want to but because he does not have that intellectual faculty to understand. I know why he is careless. He is careless does not mean that he seriously does not care us. He cares us only that much that he can care. He does not have that intellect, he is somehow capricious. He is very naive sometimes, he can not get out of his own limitations. I do not know whether he has tried or not. Even he has not tried if I presume, I am not very surprised, rather I felt it is quite intrinsic. And now if I go and make him understand all these, it may get him an adverse effect. My mother said what happened, how he always show contempt even on a simple thing done by her which is not liked by him. He immediately starts quarrelling. Today it had reached to such an extreme level through quarrelling that she became very irritated.

"I have endured enough. For 20 years I have lived with a beast. Not a single thing he has given me except inflicting pain. I have endured Enough. Now I want divorce. See yourself now, you must ask your father why he does these, why he can't talk peacefully. Ask him for better behaviour. Otherwise this is the end."

I am trapped. Sometimes I contemplate why they do not have an understanding between themselves. I don't want to intervene between them. But it is impossible for now to not intervene. Ofcourse I didn't intervene when they were quarrelling in the dinner table. And when they were splitting food on the floor. I didn't come up with the thought that how many children with the food could be fed instead I thought about how ludicrous it will look to see that how both of them will clean the floor afterwards negotiating each other. Well, I told myself to let go on, it can not be called that they are screaming, their pitch should be higher to prohibit every bird from sleeping peacefully. It always happens to me that I am offered only one time peace, either you enjoy your day and spend your night in chaos or you are pitted against something, of external factors, in the day time, for which your day goes wild. But in the night there is peace, a hand of my mother will caress me and lull me to dreamy sleep.

That night was different, my mother has already gone to bed but my father with his fatherly voice stated something which again sparkled the fragile matchstick. What happened next is really *'gharer katha'*, can not be told.

IV

Well, I may show you what happened next. You can really ask why I didn't tell you what he did when he was alone at home. I do not want to let you know because he is my lover. I really enjoy looking at him. Only in that little time I am completely left alone with my lover. He does not even know that I was there. I am telling you this but he should not know.

"Never you put off the gas cylinder." (in an irritating tone)

"You can put it off too."

"You forget it everyday to do."

"Hey, what do your 'everyday' mean? How many days you have put it off?"

"Hey, what have I said *hann*, that you are screaming on the top of your voice?"

"I am screaming or you are screaming! Not a single day has passed that you remembered to put off light, fan, or T.V. after you left the room. And now you're telling me like a monk who takes every steps consciously."

"Yes, scream, shout on the top of your voice. The person who can do nothing, speaking in such tone. (Raising his hand) I'll show you now."

"Beware, remind you, you will have to eat the rice of prison. Do not do such mistake. My life has got rotten for you."

"yes, it's me, diseased-born you, why don't you die, die and deliver me. I feel like someday I'll kill myself after I kill you."

He was still upto this point. But after hearing his father a thunder passed through his body. He started shouting at his father. He looks absolutely furious like a demon appeared with no human sensibilities, making tremors like nothing matters to him. What I can remember from his incomprehensible words are---

"You are lucky enough that you are not caught and beaten by *maa* now as you did to her previously."

And then,

"It will be good for you that you care for her and keep a peaceful contract within yourselves because know it that it'll be your last day in this house after my *maa* dies."

And for next three to four days his father completely maintained silence with him even when he started talking to her, he didn't even say a word to his son."

V

" You all are using me, I'm your money-making machine, I'm at the yolk of your service."

Something messy always happen in our home. I'm the little thing who gets blamed from both sides. When that persons there you can take it for granted that my mother will show contempt, feel irritated, and scream now and then. You can even hear a leaf falling on the ground when that person goes for work.

After I have completed my homework given by a teacher from college on a text, I sat with the script I was writing. I forgot some of it that's why I started reading it.

"Everybody has stories to tell. So do I."

Before I could complete reading, my mother started calling me for lunch.

LUNCH TABLE

"I sometimes feel jealous looking at you."

"Why?"

" You are lucky enough you know. You have a good mother who cares for you. I didn't have. We were left alone. After we get married we both were shunned away from our families. It's you I was pregnant with when this happened. One of your Baba's *maalik* advised your father to leave home immediately otherwise there shall be a big harm either to your wife or your upcoming child. I was at the bank when your father turned up said we do not have to take loan. 'We are leaving.' On that night we left. Your *amma* even sent some *gundas* to murder your father. She had the plan that when on the *'Payla Baisakh'* your father will get a large sum amount, she will seize it and then we'd be shooed away. However it didn't happen. We're living in a rental house for some time. Then the other people lives in that house got irritated after you born. Because you know, you were too naughty. You were never learnt to walk, you crawled and you had never walked, you just used to run, and everybody would run behind you so that they can catch you if you fall. I had to always tell you something.

"What did I do that they got disturbed?"

" Not once you know, everyday, after you are woken up from your nap at 4 PM, you would play on the tin door, making big sound. At this time the landowner's family used to get a nap. Often there was a quarrel because of you. They had a girl and you both were made to sleep beside each other, under the separate mosquito net. But you were a *saytan*, neither you slept nor you let that girl sleep. And you did this sort of ... Ah, *kumror chhechki!* Do I give you *dal*?"

"Yup, you have cooked this really good."

" For your *saytani*, your father told me that we have to look for our own house. But it is for you that we are in a house of our own. We did not have any moto then of making our own home. It is also true that if your *dadu* would not put his hand in this land issue, we both had to live in footpath today. Your *dadu* was very firmon the fact that the land must belong to his daughter. Your father did not have that power to go against it. But your *dadu* was very cunning and deceptive too."

I know what my mother will tell me next. But what she said that day was a few, I would rather tell you that in few details.

She didn't have a good childhood. From class eight she has to do everything on her own, she could go to study after she would finish every household activities. She used to doze off in the evening in the study time. She was tired after her rigorous work. Yet she could make out to top in the examination

Girl child delinquency is very much evident.

Her mother and her brother would beat her up sometimes, without any reasons. From class ten, she had to earn to manage her spending on her study. *Dadu* once exclaimed that he would rather put his throat on lines instead of seeing his daughter earning, he can not bear this shame (ofcourse, train lines were near the house and inhabitants of that area could only talk of this for doing this sort of things). My mother now tells me that when her brother was creating scenes with a girl that did not bring him any shame rather his daughter was doing something for herself was for him his honor is at stake. She didn't have any umbrella or special shoe for going college. She did not even have any tuition teachers. She had to walk the distance from her home to college. She was second in her college.

It makes me proud that she did, struggling with all these. A great fighter. For this I hate myself sometimes, perhaps I am not the son she deserves, who is lazy, always so *kuchu kuchu*, well...

She was married off as soon they were proposed, without considering the status quo or the upbringing if the bridegroom. She was a post graduate and she had to marry someone who is not even eight pass. She did not know at the time of her wedding ofcourse. Later she learnt the intention of the in-laws and husband of marrying her. They chose a girl from rich family, an educated so that she could reimburse their debt by getting into a job. They were only after money and property of her and her family. When she went to the house of her in-laws where she had to cook the meal of whole family, more than ten members, there she had her miscarriage. Later I was born, actually her second child, born almost twenty six days before I was expected. But I was not a premature baby. I had not been taken to child-care unit. I was alright and delivered and so loud I cried that my *baba* and *mama* heard it from outside of the nursing home and they rushed in.

For all these I can swell my biceps for a minute or two.

But my mother had not eaten anything for two days before she delivered me. It is the delinquency from both sides, from the side of my *dadu's* family as well as from my father's side. Though my father has never cared about my *maa*, it is a rare surprise I heard that a husband has never gifted anything to his wife for twenty years. She worked and earned by herself. My mother never showed any anguish and angst until I am mature enough to understand. I get even surprised that my mother has never beaten me when I was small, even when I was doing all sorts of *saytani*. Ofcourse I did not notice and realise what my mother has been going through. My childhood has gone well. I am really lucky that I have got such a mother. My mother has never beaten me for she was enraged on my father. She used to take all the big decisions. My father does not possess any intellect that he could manage anything. I can remember once my mother was telling my father why they have to postpone our house construction. Otherwise it would affect my ongoing study. It would not be right to give least attention on studies. My father simply said 'do not babble much. My head aches!"

He does not have any sense or sensibilities. If he had, he could have understood *maa*. She was taken in a hospital of Southern India where the doctor said to him, 'your wife seems to be of poor family, she has suffered from malnutrition.' Even the doctors here prescribed her all vitamins, calcium of sixty thousand power. Well, my mother is not of poor family. Their ancestors were businessmen. My *dadu* is an electrician, had three shops at *Boubaazar*. They are traditionally called *'sonar bene'(Gold merchant)* and see, how they deprived the girl for being a girl and forced her to live a life of poor. I can remember I was always discriminated by my *dadu, didun, mama, mami,* and all for being the child frompoorfamily. My *mama* has a daughter, but he is okay about it, even he loves her very much. They act very elitist. When dadu would take both of us around, he would give her a big chocolate and offer me a candy of not more than one rupee. I was happy at that time but now I can understand. There are several politics he had done with my mother. He used to take money from my mother and forbade her to say anything to anyone about it. He used to behave such that he is the one who is benefitting us by offering money. He used to give me gifts by taking money from my *maa*. Love can be bought too, learn how she has bought it for me. Nobody has ever known it. All know that he has gifted us the house but it is in the very contrary. By making these types of pronouncements he has justified his Will in the name of his son that he has given enough to his daughter and it suffices. Even *baba* also does not know these. As my *baba* is not a good person to believe in, my *maa* has never said to anyone else except me.

"It is you I am looking forward to. You are physically grown but the day you will be grown financially, you should take it that I'm emancipated. I can not spoil your life. I have been living in this condition only because of you. I do not need your support when you'll be grown. I do not expect you to do anything for me. But I can claim this is my son, I am his mother. How proud I shall be. I'll show them I'm not the nincompoop they think I was. Can you remember Raktim? Raktim is now buying new jewelleries of gold, diamond, platinum for her. She looks happy when she comes to office now. She has become healthy than she was previously. She has even bought a flat on fourteenth floor, total of eighty four lakhs. Could you imagine! Promise me son you'll study hard, you'll do something worth to mention. I don't want to be like her, she can not tell where her son works. She only says company but which company she doesn't know."

I always feel so pressurised and these are what I have always felt shits. I hate these. I hate these. I know what he did is a big achievement for them but my *maa* always notices others, and tries to put me into those criteria. Well, he is not in any way the scale by which I shall be measured. No one can be set as a scale to measure me. She knows that I have my own ambitions and aspirations yet she acts like this. It is not like I can not understand my mother, I know her insecurities and all yet she should trust me.

He had lost his father when he was only six years old. They had gone through a very tough time. Their usual breakfast is *muri chhatu,* highest *pauruti* and *ghugni* and milk for Raktimda specially. It is breakfast but foods were stretched to noon and afternoon for having lunch and snacks. It would have become their dinner too if she is tired to cook anything. Their best food dishes were *dimer jhol bhat.* She had to run her family by lending money from one another and she reimbursed that debt by lending some from another person. She had to go on like this. However, Raktimda managed to get free education in both school and college. In masters he got a job through placement. I am in better position than he was.

VI

IN THE EVENING

He is perhaps finally adding something to his script---
"Everybody has stories to tell. So do I."

He was perhaps fantasizing about his own freedom. What he will do after getting into service, what he will buy, how he would go into a love relationship, how he would also give attention to his artistic excellences. Suddenly he was stopped from the thought of what if he can not make it into any service. The first and foremost thought came in as answer of it is committing suicide. But no, he can not do it. He has thought it time and again. It scares him, freezes him for a moment. He hates this thing and specially when he thinks of his mother. How alone she would become. He hates it because he can imagine how his mother will look helpless and she would struggle to get his body to the closest of her heart and he would be caressed by all her sympathies, love, rage, fury. How every meaning of her whole life will shatter.

He immediately retreats from the thoughts of dying.

"*Dustu,* come and eat the mangoes."

"No, I'll not eat now."

"No, come eat now, if you delay you have to clean the floor after eating."

"No, I'll not eat now."

"When you'll have *dasyus,* you'll understand, you are *dustu,* and you'll have *dasyu. You're giving* so much pain to your *maa,* you will see when you will have *dasyu.*"

"No, I will not have *dasyu.*"

"No, no, you'll have *dasyu,* you will see."

"Ok, coming."

God starts existing when man suffers from insecurity. He promises time and again to God that he will study hard but it fades and becomes the part of the past as time passes.

IN PHONE

"How did it happen?"

...

"What caused this?"

...

"When did you get to know?"

...

"Where you are now? ... Come as first as you can. Where is the body now? Did they fetch it?"

...

"Ok, ok, come."

"What happened *maa* ?"

"The younger son of the *maasima* has died around 8PM."

"How?"

"How I don't know. Hari has now called your *baba* that he has died. As she has no one else to look after her, we all have to help her, he told him. Your father is now coming. I'm going now, wash the floor with water after eating."

"Ok."

She had only one physically, mentally fit son. Her elder son is a lunatic. He is more than forty years old, can do nothing much by his own. She is an old widow of more than seventy years. Her husband also died as a lunatic. She told us once that someone of her in-laws' family fed them something which drove them mad. But she had no witness. She was then pregnant with her younger son when this happened. Now when everything we presumed at the end, tragedy has already happened, we were again made to check that yes, there is something in the store still.

" I was just getting into the road, suddenly I hear *Gopaler baba* is shouting " who's there, wandering with torch?" I said "How will I go if I do not carry a torch!" With his all-known tone of barbarousness he said "How did you get the news, we have not even known fully, how could you?" I just told him "there are persons to let us know." He thought we live in a corner, they do not talk to us as well then how we could get informed! They do not know that we do not talk to them. Everyone talks with us except them, see, they were coming to collect some fees to help her, and he didn't give a single rupee. Even none of this lane appeared in her door, you know, they are jealous of her ten thousand monthly pension. Think of how narrow mentality people we live with! Your father has come. He will be going to the crematorium. No one is going except your father and another person. Have you seen her?"

"No, how can I?"

"She is not even crying, she is just saying that her neighbour cursed her son to die and finally he has died today. She is laughing you know, she seems as she is made up of stone. It will be absolutely dawn when father will be coming back. You do have college tomorrow."

"Yes…"

"Then sleep after having dinner, I would wake you up at 6AM."

VII

"If you can remember what G. B. Shaw has said, that there are seven hundred '*Philistins*', two hundred and ninety nine 'idealist', and only one 'realist'. Here Nora is the 'lone realist' who is pitted against the other two ninety nine 'idealist'. Here Nora's journey has been from an idealist to a realist. Nora was expecting that there would be a 'miracle of miracle', which is, her husband would heroically sacrifice himself; she will then kill herself in a reciprocal sacrifice. However when Torvald says that he can not "sacrifice his honour even for the person he loves" she understands that she has passed from her father's hand to his. She immediately encounters and says "millions of women have done it". She makes a very prominent remark here that she has been a "doll-wife" as she used to be her father's "doll-child". If you think on it analytically that the prefix, the 'doll' has not changed. It denotes that the status quo of the person has not changed. What is changed, the role, the role that she has to enact. So the slamming of the door does not only mean that she is getting out of the Helmar household leaving everything behind. It symbolises the fact that Nora, who has been a doll, who was enacting the roles that society ascribes, is leaving those covers behind and getting out of the "gilded cage". Public domain is full of uncertainty indeed but it is important for Nora to get out and to emerge as an 'Ibsenian New Woman'."

"Ma'am, I have a question."

"Yes"

"What we see, specifically in European cinemas that the either of the parents is parting and children are left alone and that loneliness is becoming the trauma. Is Nora's leaving a final solution? Do you not think it will be a very selfish act to do? Don't you think Nora's leaving is very instinctive?"

"Ask your girlfriends. Ask"

(Stays silent)

"Do you think the responsibility of the children are only of the mother?"

"But can we not try to change the persons like Torvald?"

"See, there is no ground for negotiation between Nora and Torvald. Remember I said you that after the enactment of the play, later, court had given verdict that a woman has the right to leave her husband's house if she pleases to do. See in _Candida,_ Candida had that ground to say things, make her husband understand. And husband too had understood that yes, he can not do anything much without her support. But here, Nora does not have that ground of understanding, when she spoke her husband still not understood. If you think Ibsen is trying to say every woman to leave the house of their husband then it would be a misinterpretation. Do you understand?

VIII

Well, if you are here, thinking that you'll get a didactic lesson or a message, you are almost wrong. I am not here to preach something. Literature to me has mostly been the property of elitists. It manifests elitists, through an elitist's eyes. Now who are elitists? We, the readers are elitist. Elitist in the sense that we always read to find a character making something different, and how he differs from others, while we read these the book suddenly becomes page-turner with thrilling, interesting plots. The mind accelerates so fast that we forget to look into the matter or we simply ignore the matter that what led other characters to not become hero, why the other characters are so mean. Do they have their particular notions too? To fathom these we need to stop hero-worshiping. The glorification of the act done by the hero has to be stopped because what they do is not always have to be right, there is no point of generalising. What I believe in is literature is a medium through which we connect and communicate each other by our stories made with artistic excellences. It presents an alternative reality in which the representation of the characters matter and readers have to be very analytical to derive their notions instead of treating it for just fun and entertainment.

You know, I have upcoming examinations and much bigger the reason than this is I have to study hard to get in into a service I dream of. I can not let you, my imaginary existence, to peep into my life, and become acquainted and go parallel to the eyes by which everything is seen. However, upto this point, if you feel in some way that I am biased, partial, and pressurising my mother to an extent directly and indirectly, you are not wrong. How can I live with a person who I hardly like, who I feel hardly close to? It is only my mother who cares for me and I also deeply acknowledge her. Before I just put an end to our relationship I want to tell you that you know only that much, you are allowed to know, not beyond. The story I was writing ends here.

PART B

To My Missing Señorita

I cannot live with you;

For the ephemerality in existence.

I cannot live without you;

For the perenniality of thoughts.

☙

World was in halt

When you, beside I

–and then there were none,

To my notice there were few

Who stayed.

☙

Several have crowded

In one gap– but still

One more gap to fill in.

World is running; I flowed

Leaving you.

&

A different you may have emerged.

But you stopped; and I

Took you from there.

I cannot see you; dream you,

But you stayed.

&

Oppo, climactic amiability

To the suave *amor*

Altered since you– dry ice.

I made you in poem; I'll be late.

Pardon me.

The Engine of 'I'

Life starts in *in-medias-res*—

When abrupt bumps shake;

Unconscious withdraws,

Naiveté— which was all,

alters.

Synonyms of understand

Breeds in.

༄

Childhood brims with stories—

Becomes stories.

Later in the dark exhausted hands

Fumble to grab the shards.

It remains when it's thought it's gone.

༄

Obstructed

In the oblivion—

Dementors are seen hovering over;

The generations make generations;

In between life is born.

In this thread 'I' is the smallest

Word who hangs

Without knowing the end.

'I' was incorporated into

Without me in it.

Life starts

When abrupt understands bump.

Debris

I went to look into myself;

Into the core.

To know the unknown.

To see, and to select.

To consider the unconsidered.

❧

Found a desire, fluorescent,

A unique indeed.

Lies beneath everything.

But triggers; rises above sometimes.

Lied to myself; ignored.

"To be or not to be

That IS the question."

To be if I'm ready to loose,

Not to be– I can not

Stand far from everyone.

ॐ

They mend me– my psyche;

Prepared my image– not how I want.

I succumbed; but I try.

I fear; I fall; I rise and

I went to look into myself again.

Wisdom of the Tree

This tree witnessed and would witness

The shadows we have written

Poetry with, and

The people who will crowd

With our shadows and

Make signs leaving

Their shadows for the

Other shadows to huddle with.

Vista Of Conundrum

Too little but big enough

Was his heart,

Which could change

A cloud to a ship;

Several artist collaborated

In his heart

To shape the plaster of the wall

Into living beings.

Unknown to the ways of the world

Robbed of his heart–

Withered of his feather,

Lights waned;

Tore him into pieces,

Splitted he more, and

He kept his

p ie ces spre ad

a cro ss.

❧

Little late– seen a woman

Whose heart got never a shape,

But offered him with all of hers.

He acknowledged and

Made the pieces the bullets

Through her efforts.

Got bullets, but no gun!

More to proceed, more to go,

In this vista of conundrum.

Narcissus

That moment is a platform

When life halts,

Some leave, some ride in;

Compartments never go empty.

Life is too noisy,

Like the train runs

On it's tracks.

❧

But they come to visit

The particular compartments

Of their choice.

They are too busy

On themselves.

What I knew was them,

Why they came.

The beauties I possessed,

–Sucked, for their use.

The piece they ignored

Was me, the colour

Unrecognised.

&

The doors I opened

From the word that's lone

For I knew the reason I'm alone.

Now 'arrogant' is the word for 'I'

As they can not make out.

'I' is the word who

Interests me.

'I' is the shell on which

I dive to be lost

To find the pearl in me.

For the world, I met the end

But I lived the eternity.

I live on them.

I live in every garden.

I sell my sorrows

I sell my sorrows.

Sorrows– felt through sailing boats

Across the corners of heart.

Sorrows, in a state of mute air–

Unable to take the shape of tears.

Sorrows, where I live,

The space is of sorrow.

Sorrows, where, even death

Finds hard to penetrate;

In the air so smoky.

&

I sell my sorrows.

To those who finds me

In the corners of streets,

In the showcases sometimes,

In the streets of known and unknown.

கூ

Given up on love,

Who would have given a tight hug.

Would have rested on

His shoulder through thick and thin.

But love of more value

Which is perceived of, by default,

Is a mere strategy.

Fulfilment and recuperation

Are what they call

In a word, love.

A ray of hope, a saviour,

Is not what I am.

கூ

I am a burdened soul

And burdening to them.

I see the world

Which is vacuum to me.

My soul is hardly instilled.

My skins' ripped off,

In a gradual transcendence,

That I feel blessed of nakedness;

–Relieving, into sheets, smeared with, sorrows.

Thus, I sell my sorrows,

To those who find me in them.

We will fly, will we?

Can you step out from yourself

And look at you?

Do you recognise

Where you stand?

I think– gibberish!

❧

Robotic routine with illusionary success

Binds the life

In gilded cage.

Can we step out?

–No. No perhaps.

❧

We flow processed and preserved

Like the pickles

In the jar.

Do we feel guilt if

We do not fit in?

&

We are not ours and

Mirror has failed time and again.

It does not show

The reflection of our own now.

I do not know me.

&

We have eyes, yet blind.

We see colours, but can't feel them.

Time is the prisoner of the clock

And that is in our hand.

Should we throw it?

&

I wish I could explore, venture

The subterraneous passages.

I wish I could live in solidarity;

Beneath the blue sky, in the green

With my loneliness.

℘

Tiresias would be worshipped

To find one's mad woman

In the attic.

We will fly and come back

Before the night falls.

NOT NAMED

I

A white hair in her

Last counting years

Halts in front of a lottery shop,

Bets her luck,

The luck she has saved

For years, the years

That went through the

Notes of '*tivra*' and '*komal*'.

The place was starry

But the passage

Was narrow and too dark

To see the end.

The song of life

Where *tivra* and *komals*

Make sounds

– *sargams* fall flat.

&

II

The passage resembles–

Hate is the poetic lingo

That is put as the ventilator

Between my mind and

The other slums of

Human existence.

For the scavenger though I am

Who picks the excreta

As manure to the minds.

The humans that are born

Can not become the human anymore.

But underneath the dark cover

There are the white muscles and

Coloured syrup flows in it.

The colour I extract

Colours the colour

Thus, can be used no more.

Yet, I proceed,

Try to separate the colour

From the flower.

I bet my luck once more

If the colours are produced

Arrayed in a manner,

Looks beautiful.

III

The passage resembles–

Sometimes *sargams* make sounds too.

When a bubble of fantasy

Bubbles from nowhere

In a calm surface of water.

Calm is a sign, an ominous.

For I harbour a 'he'.

The heat I feel,

For the heat I know I have.

He, I design everytime different

For the hunger I feel.

He lingers, I feel sucked;

For a moment I live in him.

When time leaves me

I masturbate him out.

The storm never comes

Though the sign it made.

The storm will be swirled

When I can impose

My 'he' upon the 'he' that arrives;

When we could feel cold

By the heat we shared.

The heat in me shivers

For the wave of heat

That blows outside.

୧

IV

The passage resembles–

I, the witness of only two decades

But the past I lived with

Not of two decades.

The two bins I got,

I often slipped into them;

The bins –full of waste;

The waste of ills received.

I smell of them.

The poems in my life

Comes non-metrical.

'Tivra' and *'komals'* are dominant

In which *sargams*

Make occasional appearance.

The passage in which

My life is travelling through

Is not named in history.

Neither it's new nor unique

But because it's silent.

The sound it's make

–Ignored before it's reached.

Aspiration is a mortal being.

It seduces, me too.

Enjoying in a lovely intercourse.

I'll be Arjun to shoot

The arrow that penetrates only the eye.

The luck if dismissed

I shall fall like Icarus

That gifted him no existence.

But the non-existent 'I'

Will be multiplied.

More the passing of wind through

The ventilator could be heard.

&

The horn makes sound nearby,

I passed the old lady behind.

"where to" – auto stops,

Leg crumples– " there,

On that way".

GLOSSARY

PART- A

Maa- Mother

Baba- Father

Maalik- Owner

Gundas- Gangster, Hooligan

Payla Baisakh- First day of first Bengali month, *Baisakh*. Beginning of Bengali New Year

Amma- paternal grandmother

Saytan- The devil

Kumror chhechki- a delicious dish, made up with pumpkin

Dal- Lentil soup

Saytani- Mischief

Dadu- Maternal grandfather

Kuchu kuchu- Affectionate calling

Muri chhatu- Puffed rice with gram flour

Pauruti- Bread

Ghugni- Dish of curried wholeyellow peas.

Dimer jhol bhat- Rice, with a sort of egg curry.

Dustu- Naughty

Dasyu- Pirate

Maasima- Sisterof one's mother. Use to call aged persons affectionately

PART B

Suave- soft

Amor- love

In-medias-res- begins from the middle of the things

Naivéte- naive

Dementors- creatures taken from *Harry Potter series*, who deprive human minds of happiness and intelligence.

Tiresias- a blind prophet of Apollo in Greek mythology.

Komal- soft or flat notes in Indian classical music.

Tivra- *Madhyam* is the only sharp note in Indian classical music.

Sargam- an acronym created by combining the first four syllables (*sa, re, ga, ma,*).

Arjun- mythological character from *Mahabharata,* only who could shot the targeted eye of a bird when Dronacharya asked both the *Pandavaas* and *Kauravas* to shoot the target.

Icarus- tragicfigurefromGreek mythology, who died for his high aspiration, for flying close to the sun with wings of wax made by his father.

Soumya Adhikari was born in 2001 in West Bengal, India. He is a student of English Literature. He graduated with honours from Bhairab Ganguly College, affiliated with West Bengal State University, in 2022. He completed his Higher Secondary Education at Jawahar Navodaya Vidyalaya, Banipur. This is his debut book.